Thanksgiving AT Our House

Wendy Watson

Clarion Books·New York

For my sisters,
who know how to celebrate.

Calligraphy on cover and title page by Paul Shaw.

Clarion Books
a Houghton Mifflin Company imprint
215 Park Avenue South, New York, NY 10003
Printed in the USA

Library of Congress Cataloging-in-Publication Data
Watson, Wendy.
Thanksgiving at our house / Wendy Watson.
p.   cm.
Summary: The family busily prepares for Thanksgiving and
has a grand feast with visiting relatives. Includes
Thanksgiving poems.
ISBN 0-395-53626-X   PA ISBN 0-395-69944-4
[1. Thanksgiving Day—Fiction.   2. Family life—
Fiction.]   I. Title.
PZ7.W332Th   1991
[E]—dc20   90-26138   CIP   AC

HOR   10 9 8 7 6 5 4 3

Monday—wash.
Tuesday—scour.
Wednesday—bake.
Thursday—devour.

It's Monday, and Thanksgiving is coming!

Pussycat, pussycat, where have you been?
I've been to see Grandmother over the green!
What did she give you? Milk in a can.
What did you say for it? Thank you, Grandam!

Today is Tuesday.
We gather onions and turnips at Grandma's farm.
We buy the turkey at the store.

Now it's Wednesday.
We clean the whole house.
We iron our party clothes.
We wash the fancy dishes.
Aunt Em and Uncle John and Susie will come today
from Idaho.

Here we go round the bramble bush, the bramble bush, the bramble bush. Here we go round the bramble bush, On a cold frosty morning!

This is the way we clean our rooms,

Clean our rooms, clean our rooms. This is the way we clean our rooms, On a cold frosty morning!

This is the way we wash our clothes, Wash our clothes, wash our . . .

This little pig had a scrub-a-scrub,
This little pig had a rub-a-dub,
This little pig-a-wig ran upstairs,
This little pig-a-wig called out, "Bears!"
Down came the jar with a loud Slam! Slam!
And this little pig had all the jam.

It's Thursday, Thanksgiving Day!
We get up early.
The turkey is already roasting.
We take baths and put on our party clothes.

Here are Grandma and Grandpa!
And our cousins from New York,
and Aunt Mary who lives by the sea.
George and Maude will come from over the mountain.
They will bring the pies.

Clap hands, Grandpa comes,
With his pocket full of plums,
And a cake for Johnny.

We all decorate the whole house.
We make place cards and turkeys,
and hang up corn.
Kitty helps.
But where are George and Maude?

The kitchen is full of people.
Good smells are everywhere.
No, doggie—that's not for you!
Now Dad has to go to the store for more butter.
Is the turkey done?
Hurry—we're hungry!

As I went up the apple tree,
All the apples fell on me;
Bake a pudding, bake a pie,
Did you ever tell a lie?

Onion's skin very thin,
Mild winter coming in.
Onion's skin thick and tough,
Coming winter cold and rough.

Davy Davy Dumpling,
Boil him in the pot;
Sugar him and butter him,
And eat him while he's hot.

Nose, nose, jolly red nose,
And what gave thee that jolly red nose?
Nutmeg and ginger, cinnamon and cloves,
That's what gave me this jolly red nose.

Hey ding a ding,
What shall I sing?
How many holes in a skimmer?
Four-and-twenty,
My plate's empty;
Pray, Mama, give us our dinner.

Everything is ready.

Just in time, here come George and Maude!

They're *always* late.

Now we can begin.

We like to sing our Thanksgiving grace.

Grandpa is loud!

We eat for a long time.
Aunt Mary makes more gravy.
Everyone tells stories.
We brag about how many pieces of pie we've eaten.

Piping hot, smoking hot,
What I've got,
You know not,
Hot hot pease, hot, hot, hot;
Hot are my pease, hot.

Robin the Bobbin, the big-bellied
Ben, He ate more meat than
fourscore men; He ate
a cow, he ate a calf,
He ate a butcher
and a half,
He ate a church,
he ate a steeple,
He ate the priest
and all the
people!

Robert Rowley rolled a round roll round,
A round roll Robert Rowley rolled round;
Where rolled the round roll
Robert Rowley rolled round?

Apple pie,
apple pie,
Peter likes apple pie;
So do I, so do I.

Bye, baby bumpkin,
Where's Tony Lumpkin?
My lady's on her deathbed,
With eating half a pumpkin.

Dull November brings the blast;
Then the leaves are whirling fast.

After dinner, some people take naps,
but we go outdoors.
It is dark.
Snowflakes are falling.

When we come in, the house is warm.
We play games.
Some people wash dishes.
Some people even eat again!

Bo-peep
Little Bo-peep
Now's the time
For hide and seek.

A riddle, a riddle,
As I suppose;
A hundred eyes,
And never a nose.

A duck and a drake,
A nice barley cake,
With a penny to pay the old baker,
A hop and a scotch,
A hop and a scotch,
Slitherum, slatherum, take her.

March, march, head erect,
Left, right, that's correct.

Ride a cock-horse
To Banbury Cross,
To see what Tommy can buy;
A penny white loaf,
A penny white cake,
And a two-penny apple pie.

One's none;
Two's some;
Three's many;
Four's a penny;
Five's a little hundred.

At last everyone goes home—
all except Aunt Em and Uncle John and Susie.
They will stay another day.

In the morning we can have cold turkey and pumpkin pie
for breakfast,
but now it's time for bed.
Good night.

WENDY WATSON comes from a family that has produced several generations of professional authors and artists. She was raised with seven brothers and sisters on a farm in Vermont, where she received her early education and art training from her parents. She later studied painting in Truro, Massachusetts, and at the National Academy of Design in New York City. Ms. Watson is the author-illustrator of more than a dozen children's books and has illustrated many others.